ANIMAL INVADERS: DESTROYING NATIVE HABITATS

ATTACK OF THE BULLFROGS

BY THERESE SHEA

Gareth Stevens PUBLISHING

Please visit our website, www.garethstevens.com. For a free color catalog of all our high-quality books, call toll free 1-800-542-2595 or fax 1-877-542-2596.

Cataloging-in-Publication Data

Names: Shea, Therese.
Title: Attack of the bullfrogs / Therese Shea.
Description: New York : Gareth Stevens Publishing, 2017. | Series: Animal invaders: destroying native habitats | Includes index.
Identifiers: ISBN 9781482456578 (pbk.) | ISBN 9781482456660 (library bound) | ISBN 9781482456646 (6 pack)
Subjects: LCSH: Bullfrog–Juvenile literature.
Classification: LCC QL668.E27 2017 | DDC 597.8'92–dc23

First Edition

Published in 2017 by
Gareth Stevens Publishing
111 East 14th Street, Suite 349
New York, NY 10003

Designer: Laura Bowen
Editor: Kristen Nelson

Photo credits: Cover, pp. 1 (bullfrog), 15 Joe McDonald/Corbis Documentary/Getty Images; cover, pp. 1–24 (background) arigato/Shutterstock.com; cover, pp. 1–24 (corners) Gala/Shutterstock.com; cover, pp. 1–24 (title bar) drada/Shutterstock.com; pp. 1–24 (caption box) Amovitania/Shutterstock.com; p. 5 Bruce MacQueen/Shutterstock.com; p. 7 Waring Abbott/Michael Ochs Archives/Getty Images; p. 8 feathercollector/Shutterstock.com; p. 9 Darren J. Bradley/Shutterstock.com; p. 10 Paul S. Wolf/Shutterstock.com; p. 11 Chris E. Heisey/Shutterstock.com; p. 17 (both) Chris McGrath/Getty Images News/Getty Images; p. 19 E R DEGGINGER/Science Source/Getty Images; p. 20 George Grail/National Geographic/Getty Images; p. 21 JIANG HONGYAN/Shutterstock.com.

Printed in the United States of America

CPSIA compliance information: Batch #CW17GS: For further information contact Gareth Stevens, New York, New York at 1-800-542-2595.

CONTENTS

Words in the glossary appear in **bold** type the first time they are used in the text.

QUIET DOWN!

Jug-o-rum, jug-o-rum! What's that noise? If you're near a pond or lake, it might be a bullfrog! The American bullfrog is the largest North American frog. It can weigh as much as 1 pound (0.5 kg).

Bullfrogs have a deep call, or croak, that can be heard a half mile (0.8 km) away! Some think the croak sounds like the noise a bull makes—that's how the frog got its name. That croak means trouble in some parts of the world. Read on to find out why.

FIGHT BACK WITH FACTS

A bullfrog's back legs can be 10 inches (25 cm) long. It can jump as far as 6 feet (1.8 m)!

Bullfrogs are usually green or brown with a white or yellow underside. A bullfrog's body is about 8 inches (20 cm) long.

AT HOME WITH BULLFROGS

The American bullfrog is native to the central and eastern United States and southeastern Canada. Like all frogs, bullfrogs are amphibians. They need to live in or near freshwater bodies of water. Bullfrogs like warm, calm, shallow water such as in ponds and lakes.

Only male bullfrogs make the famous bullfrog croak. They do this to draw **mates**. Mating season takes place from May to July in the North and from February to October in the South.

FIGHT BACK WITH FACTS

During mating season, male bullfrogs may have a yellow throat.

Female bullfrogs are larger than males.

A LOT OF EGGS!

The female bullfrog lays her eggs in water. She may lay close to 20,000 eggs at a time! The male bullfrog then **fertilizes** them. The eggs float on the water's surface.

When the eggs **hatch**, the bullfrog **tadpoles** live in water. Over time, they grow legs and lose their tail. It may take as long as 4 years, but the tadpoles come out of the water as adult bullfrogs. Another 2 years may pass before the bullfrogs are old enough to mate.

BULLFROG EGGS

Bullfrog tadpoles hatch about 4 days after the eggs are fertilized.

MORE SURVIVORS

Other kinds of North American frogs only lay a few thousand eggs. This might sound like a lot, but many eggs, tadpoles, and young frogs are eaten before they become adults. Bullfrogs lay many more thousands of eggs, so many more bullfrogs survive to become adults. Bullfrog eggs and tadpoles also survive because they don't taste good to many fish.

Bullfrog predators include herons, turtles, water snakes, and raccoons. People who eat frog legs may hunt bullfrogs, too!

This great egret has found itself a bullfrog snack!

SPREADING OUT

The American bullfrog has spread into the western United States, northern Canada, Mexico, and Cuba. Some of the spread was by accident. People have accidentally picked up bullfrog eggs when they've taken water from one source to fill other ponds and lakes. In other places, people introduced bullfrogs on purpose as a food source.

Bullfrogs spread naturally, too. They like to live alone and have their own territory. A territory might include from 10 to 80 feet (3 to 24 m) along the water's edge.

FIGHT BACK WITH FACTS

People brought bullfrogs to California in the 1890s to be a source of frog legs to eat.

BULLFROG RANGE

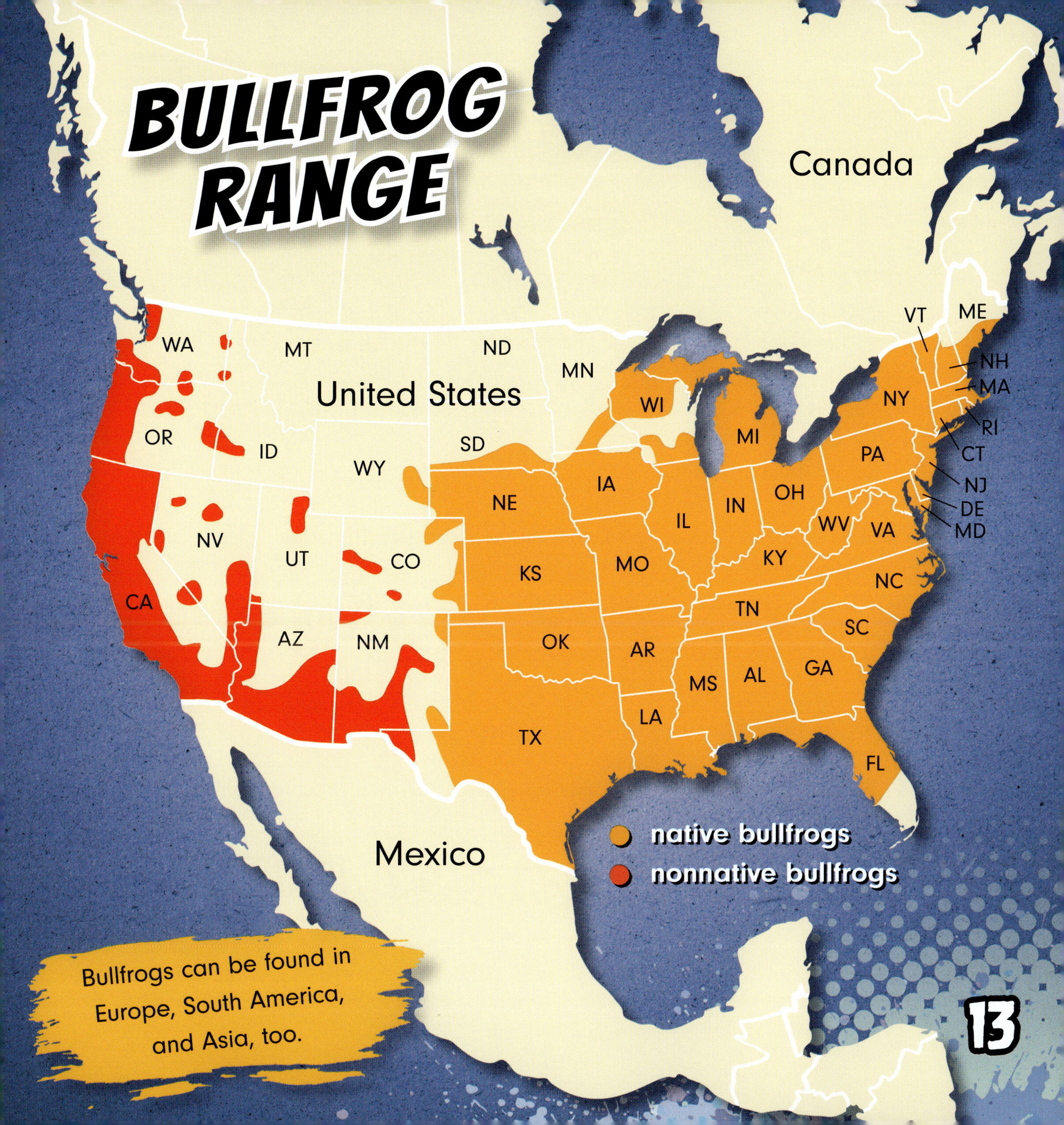

Bullfrogs can be found in Europe, South America, and Asia, too.

UNWELCOME GUESTS

Bullfrogs are an **invasive species** in nonnative **habitats**. That means they harm these habitats. They **outcompete** other animals for food, leaving less food than usual. And bullfrogs can really eat! Bullfrogs eat snakes, worms, bugs, eggs, mice, birds, and other frogs. The bullfrogs' hunger is also a problem when they eat **endangered** species.

Bullfrogs hunt at night, waiting silently for prey to pass. When something tasty comes by, they jump on it. If an animal fits in a bullfrog's mouth, it's dinner!

FIGHT BACK WITH FACTS

Bullfrogs eat other bullfrogs!

This bullfrog snacks on a worm.

SPREADING DISEASE

Bullfrogs also spread **disease**. Frogs all over the world can die from the chytrid (KY-truhd) **fungus**. It causes a skin disease that can kill amphibians in just weeks. **Infected** animals spread the fungus when they're set free in the wild or when water they've used is dumped into a lake or pond.

The bullfrog trade plays a part in the fungus's spread. Each year, more than 5 million bullfrogs are imported to New York City and to San Francisco and Los Angeles, California. Many of these bullfrogs carry the fungus and infect other frogs.

FIGHT BACK WITH FACTS

Bullfrogs at stores in several US cities were tested for the chytrid fungus. About 40 percent were infected.

Millions of bullfrogs are shipped to the United States each year as food and pets. Many people are hoping to stop this trade.

PLAN OF ACTION

In many areas of the United States and Canada, people are taking action against bullfrogs in nonnative habitats. Governments are allowing people to hunt them and collect bullfrog eggs and tadpoles. They're also introducing animals that are known to eat bullfrogs, such as largemouth bass, into the habitats. Some places have laws that make it illegal to sell, move, or keep bullfrogs.

Still, bullfrogs are very hard to control. They have so many young and can easily hop from one water source to another.

FIGHT BACK WITH FACTS

The chytrid fungus may have caused about 100 frog species to become extinct, or die out.

Bullfrogs don't have as many predators in nonnative habitats, which makes it hard to keep their population in check.

YOU CAN HELP!

According to a recent study, about one-third of all amphibian species are in danger of dying out. Reasons include habitat destruction, the chytrid fungus, and pollution. Hungry bullfrogs make things worse when they're introduced into new places.

You can help with the fight against invasive bullfrogs. Don't buy bullfrogs or bullfrog tadpoles from stores. Spread the word to neighbors who might buy bullfrogs for backyard ponds. Bullfrogs aren't all bad—they just need to stay in their own habitats!

STOP THOSE FROGS!

Do your part to prevent the spread of this invasive species!

GOAL

Stop bullfrogs from spreading into nonnative habitats.

REASONS

- Bullfrogs eat endangered species.
- Bullfrogs spread disease and the chytrid fungus to other amphibians.
- Bullfrogs outcompete other animals for food.

ACTIONS

- Stop the buying, selling, and moving of bullfrogs.
- Allow people to hunt bullfrogs in nonnative areas.
- Introduce bullfrog predators to nonnative areas.

GLOSSARY

disease: an illness that affects a person, animal, or plant

endangered: in danger of dying out

fertilize: to add male cells to a female's eggs to make babies

fungus: a growing thing that may resemble a plant but lacks green color and cannot make its own food, instead living on or in plants, animals, or dying matter

habitat: the natural place where an animal or plant lives

hatch: to break open or come out of

infect: to cause someone or something to become sick or affected by disease

invasive species: one kind of living thing likely to spread and be harmful when placed in a new area

mate: one of two animals that come together to make babies

outcompete: to be more successful at doing an action than something else

tadpole: the larva of an amphibian, such as a frog or toad

FOR MORE INFORMATION

Books

Gray, Susan H. *Bullfrog.* Ann Arbor, MI: Cherry Lake Publishing, 2009.

Latta, Sara L. *Keep Out! Invasive Species.* North Mankato, MN: Capstone Press, 2014.

Phillips, Dee. *Amphibians.* Mankato, MN: New Forest Press, 2011.

Websites

American Bullfrog
animals.nationalgeographic.com/animals/amphibians/american-bullfrog/
Hear what the bullfrog sounds like on this site.

American Bullfrog
www.biokids.umich.edu/critters/Lithobates_catesbeianus/
Discover more information about the bullfrog's life cycle.

INDEX